RACHEL MOSS (illustrator) was born in Jamaica and studied animation in England at the University for the Creative Arts. She spends her days illustrating children's books such as *Respect* with song lyrics by Otis Redding, *African* with song lyrics by Peter Tosh, *I Am a Promise* by Shelly Ann Fraser Pryce, *Abigail's Glorious Hair,* and *Milo & Myra Learn Manners with Mr. Mongoose.*

"These Boots Are Made for Walkin'"
Written by Lee Hazlewood
Courtesy of Criterion Music Corp.
Used by Permission. All Rights Reserved.

LyricPop is a children's picture book collection by LyricVerse and Akashic Books.

**lyricverse.**

Published by Akashic Books
Song lyrics ©1965 Lee Hazlewood
Illustrations ©2020 Rachel Moss

ISBN: 978-1-61775-875-1
Library of Congress Control Number: 2020935752
First printing

Printed in China

Akashic Books
Brooklyn, New York
Twitter: @AkashicBooks
Facebook: AkashicBooks
E-mail: info@akashicbooks.com
Website: www.akashicbooks.com

# These Boots Are Made for Walkin'

Song lyrics by Lee Hazlewood

Illustrations by Rachel Moss

AKASHIC BOOKS    LYRICPOP

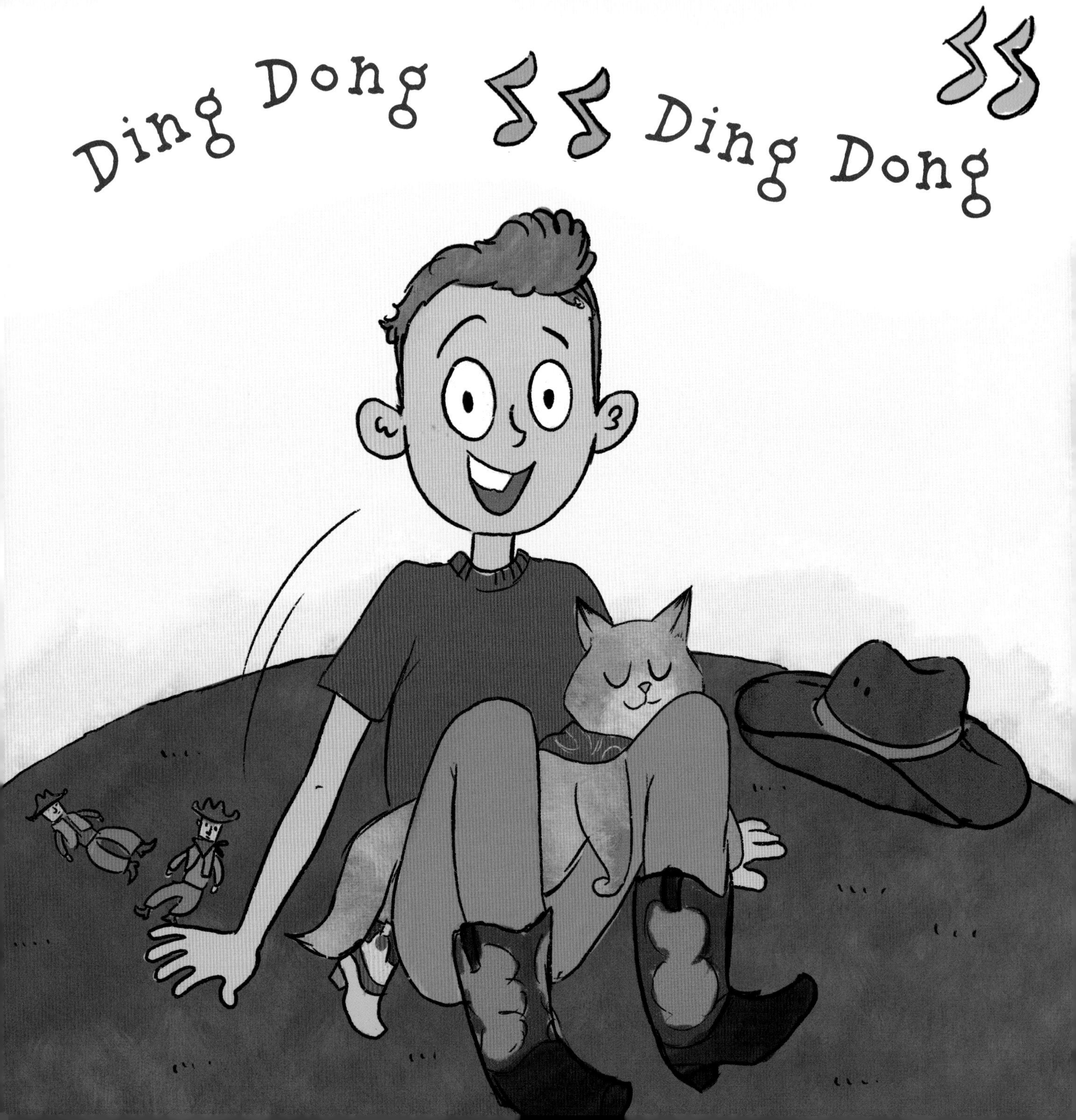
Ding Dong
Ding Dong

Somethin' you call love
but confess

You've been a'messin' where you shouldn't've been a'messin' a'messin'

And now someone else
is gettin' all your best

These boots are made
for walkin'

And that's just
what they'll do

One of these days
these boots
are gonna walk
all over you . . .

Yeah . . .

You keep lyin'
when you oughta be truthin'

And you keep losin'
when you oughta not bet

You keep samein' when you oughta be a'changin'

Now what's right is right, but you ain't been right yet

These boots are made for walkin'

And that's just what they'll do

One of these days these boots are gonna walk all over you . . .

You keep playin'
where you
shouldn't be playin'

And you keep thinkin' that you'll never get burned, HAH!

I just found me
a brand-new box
of matches,
YEAH

And what he
knows you
ain't had time
to learn

These boots are made for walkin'

And that's just what they'll do

One of these days these boots are gonna walk all over you . . .

Are you ready, boots?

Start walkin'!

# LOOK OUT FOR THESE LyricPop TITLES

**African** SONG LYRICS BY PETER TOSH
ILLUSTRATIONS BY RACHEL MOSS

**(Sittin' on) The Dock of the Bay**
SONG LYRICS BY OTIS REDDING AND STEVE CROPPER
ILLUSTRATIONS BY KAITLYN SHEA O'CONNOR

**Don't Stop** SONG LYRICS BY CHRISTINE McVIE
ILLUSTRATIONS BY NUSHA ASHJAEE

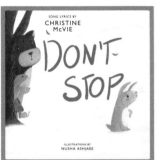

**Good Vibrations**
SONG LYRICS BY MIKE LOVE AND BRIAN WILSON
ILLUSTRATIONS BY PAUL HOPPE

**Humble and Kind** SONG LYRICS BY LORI McKENNA
ILLUSTRATIONS BY KATHERINE BLACKMORE

**Move the Crowd**
SONG LYRICS BY ERIC BARRIER AND WILLIAM GRIFFIN
ILLUSTRATIONS BY KIRK PARRISH

**Respect** SONG LYRICS BY OTIS REDDING
ILLUSTRATIONS BY RACHEL MOSS

**We Got the Beat** SONG LYRICS BY CHARLOTTE CAFFEY
ILLUSTRATIONS BY KAITLYN SHEA O'CONNOR

**We're Not Gonna Take It** SONG LYRICS BY DEE SNIDER
ILLUSTRATIONS BY MARGARET McCARTNEY

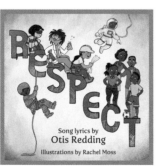